Have you ever met Mussin?

My wonderful friend!

Some grown-ups say

That he's only pretend.

Have you ever met Mussin?

Who thought it OK

To put stones in Dad's shoes

And throw his slippers away!

Have you ever met Mussin?

Who at Grandpa's barbeque,

Stole every sausage

And gave them a chew!

Have you ever met Mussin?

The funniest creature,

Who plays all sorts of tricks

To frighten my teacher!

Have you ever met Mussin?

Who as quick as a wink,

Chopped off Mum's tulips

Before she could blink.

"If I ever catch Mussin..."

Dad always shouts.

But when Mussin's in trouble

Mussin's never about!

If you're ever out walking

One bright sunny day.

You'll see Mussin out walking

The very same way.

He'll jump where you jump

And he'll skip where you skip.

He's ever so quiet

And ever so quick.

The best time to see him,
But don't make a sound,
Is when the sun's shining bright
And you look at the ground!